Pin the Ta

written by Pam Holden
illustrated by Kelvin Hawley

One Saturday, when it was too stormy to play at the park, Dad had a good idea. He thought of a game for the family to play at home. He asked the children if they knew how to play Pin the Tail on the Donkey.

"Look at this poor donkey without a tail," he said, holding up a picture of a funny-looking donkey. "How will he swish the flies away? I've found his tail. I wonder who can stick it back on for him?"

"I'll try to fix it," said Sam. "Give me the donkey's tail to hold."
Dad put a blindfold over Sam's eyes and tied it at the back of his head, so that he couldn't see anything at all.
"Turn around three times," said Dad. "Are you ready? Now go and put the tail back on the donkey."

As Sam walked slowly forward with the tail, he tried to remember where the donkey's back was. When he reached out his hand to stick the tail on, everybody started to laugh.

As soon as Dad took the blindfold off, Sam knew why they were laughing. The tail was hanging on the donkey's front leg!
"I got it wrong, didn't I?" he said in surprise.

"It's your turn, Mary," said Dad, and he handed the tail to her. After he tied the blindfold around her head, he turned her slowly around.
The other children counted, "One, two, three."
All the family laughed when Mary stuck on the tail because she left it hanging on the donkey's ear!

John took the tail next, but he stuck it right on the poor donkey's nose.
"That's funny! It's at the wrong end!" shouted the other children.
Zoe had a quick turn because she didn't like wearing the blindfold. She hurried forward and stuck the tail in the middle of the donkey's tummy!

Liz said, "It's my turn. I'll fix that poor donkey." She held the tail in her hand, while Dad tied the blindfold tightly over her eyes.

"Now I can't see anything at all!" said Liz. "Where's the donkey?"

Just then the phone began to ring, so Dad quickly turned her around three times before he hurried to answer the phone.

"Ring, ring! Ring, ring!" went the phone again.
While Dad picked it up to talk to his friend,
Liz walked slowly forward to find the donkey.

But she put the tail in the wrong place, too.
Liz didn't stick it anywhere on the donkey at all.
She missed him, and she stuck the tail on Dad!

"Why are you all laughing?" asked Dad, as he put down the phone. The children pointed at his back. "That's funny — I've turned into a donkey!" he said. "Hee haw! Hee haw!"

Are you a Word Whiz?

- **ph**one
- **ph**oto
- **ph**otogra**ph**
- tele**ph**one
- **ph**ones
- **ph**otos

How many new words can you make from these?

end   f**ix**   st**ick**   h**ang**   h**old**

Fluency Level 3
Fiction Set A

GUIDED READING	R/R INTERVENTION	LEXILE MEASURE
J	19	530L

Red Rocket™ Readers

Engineered by Flying Start Books

redrocketreaders.com

ISBN 978-1-887506-09-3